·T·H·E·
WHITE SWAN EXPRESS

A Story About Adoption

by **JEAN DAVIES OKIMOTO** and **ELAINE M. AOKI**
Illustrated by **MEILO SO**

Clarion Books · New York

For Elaine and Dennis—J. D. O.

For Emily—E. M. A.

For Holly Shang Juan—M. S.

Clarion Books
a Houghton Mifflin Company imprint
215 Park Avenue South, New York, NY 10003
Text copyright © 2002 by Jean Davies Okimoto and Elaine M. Aoki
Illustrations copyright © 2002 by Meilo So

Library of Congress Cataloging-in-Publication Data
Okimoto, Jean Davies.
The White Swan express : a story about adoption / by Jean
Davies Okimoto and Elaine Aoki ; illustrated by Meilo So.
p. cm.
Summary: Across North America, people in four different homes prepare for
a special trip to China, while four baby girls in China await their
new adoptive parents.
ISBN 0-618-16453-7
[1. Intercountry adoption—Fiction. 2. Adoption—Fiction.
3. Babies—Fiction. 4. China—Fiction.] I. Aoki, Elaine Mei.
II. So, Meilo, ill. III. Title.
PZ7.O415 Wf 2002
[E]—dc21   2002005983

TWP 10 9 8 7 6 5 4 3

The sun rose above North America, and all over the continent people were getting up. For some of them it was a special day.

3

In Miami, in the pink stucco house on Everglade Avenue, Beth Maynard was sound asleep. But Lewis Maynard was awake. He sat by the window waiting for dawn. When the sun came up, he looked at his watch, then looked at his wife and burst into song. "It's a beautiful day—hey! hey! hey! To be on our way—yeah! yeah! yeah!" Beth opened her eyes and sat up in bed.

Ring-ring-ring-ring went the little clock in the yellow house on Vashon Island near Seattle, Washington. But Andrea Lee and Charlotte Appleford were already awake. They'd been up for hours watching the sun rise over the Cascade Mountains.

In Minnetonka, Minnesota, in the downstairs of the duplex on Ashland Avenue, the clock radio clicked and on came a song. "Oh, happy day!" sang the radio. Rebecca Mandel smiled, then hugged her cat, Ralph, and leaped out of bed.

In Canada, on Willowdale Street in Toronto, Ontario, the alarm clock beeped in apartment 3C. Jessica and Howard Suzuki cuddled and kissed, and then jumped out of bed.

5

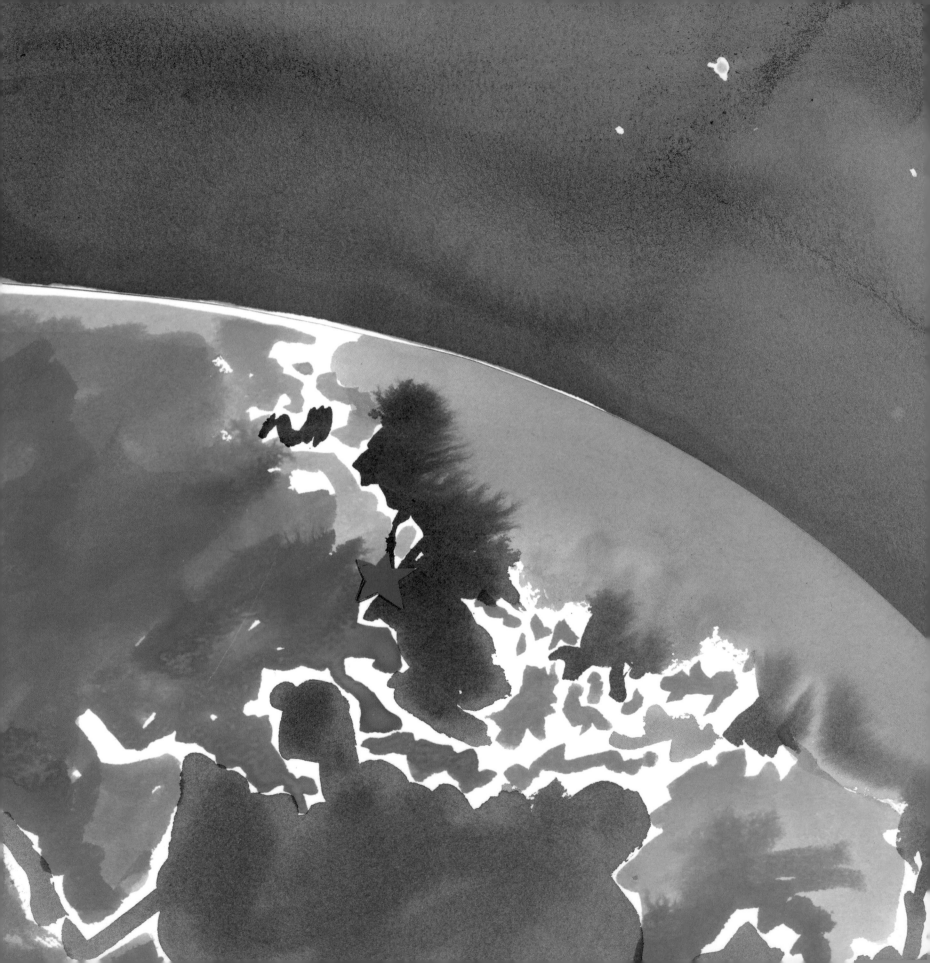

On the other side of the world the moon rose over the continent of Asia.

For some who were very young and very small, a special day was coming soon.

In the city of Guangzhou in the province of Guangdong, in China, the moon shone through the orphanage window. Four baby girls dressed exactly alike slept in their cribs.

Wu Li slept on her back with her arms stretched wide like the branches of a tree.

Li Shen snuggled on her side.

Qian Ye slept curled in a ball.

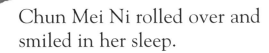

Chun Mei Ni rolled over and smiled in her sleep.

8

Still asleep, Wu Li smacked her lips,

Li Shen burped,

Qian Ye yawned,

and Chun Mei Ni snored.

9

Across the world in North America the sun rose higher in the sky.

In Miami, Beth Maynard soaked in the tub and in the kitchen Lewis Maynard burned the toast.

On Vashon Island, Andrea Lee put the kettle on for tea while Charlotte Appleford brushed her teeth.

In Minnetonka, Rebecca Mandel ate a grapefruit and fed Ralph.

In Toronto, Howard Suzuki sang in the shower while Jessica dried her hair.

10

Then they dressed and packed. They looked at their lists and checked their bags. There were diapers and baby carriers, knitted hats and blankets. There were bibs and baby food, and booties and warm sweaters. There were burp cloths, cans of formula, and little panda bears. There were baby wipes and medicine and bottles and spoons.

And there were papers—lots of important papers—and baby pictures as tiny as a stamp.

They checked the bags and checked the papers, and then they checked them again. Finally, they were ready. The time had come.

They went to the airports and stood in long lines,

showed their tickets, and boarded the planes.

They found their seats, took off their coats, stored their bags,

and fastened their seatbelts.

All across North America the planes took off. Up over Toronto, over Seattle, Miami, and Minneapolis/St. Paul. High over the clouds, the seven travelers were on their way.

To China.

12

On the very long trip, most of them slept and ate several meals—except for Lewis Maynard, who was too excited and only wanted peanuts.

Andrea Lee wrote in her journal, "I wonder if Li Shen will cry when I hold her. Will I be able to comfort her?" Next to her, Charlotte Appleford looked out at the clouds, closed her eyes, and said silently, *Thank you for this day.*

Rebecca Mandel read a book called *What to Expect the First Year.*

Jessica Suzuki listened to a tape and practiced the words she would say.

"*Wo shi ni de mama,*" she whispered, "I am Mommy. *Wo ai ni,*" she said softly. "I love you."

Howard Suzuki looked at the photo of Chun Mei Ni and wondered if she would love him.

As night fell, the planes got closer to China.

A few hours later the pilots announced that it was time to get ready for landing.

Lewis and Beth Maynard held hands. So did Andrea Lee and Charlotte Appleford. Rebecca Mandel said a prayer. Jessica and Howard Suzuki held their photo of Chun Mei Ni. *"Wo shi ni de mama,"* Jessica whispered.

All their hearts pounded.

They were very tired when they arrived in China, but they still had farther to go. Now the travelers from Toronto, Vashon Island, Miami, and Minnetonka became a group, trading stories and showing each other their tiny photos.

14

Together they boarded a bus and set out for Guangzhou, the city where they would meet their daughters.

They passed factories and villages, and cities with shops. Everything was covered with dense gray fog.

When they got to Guangzhou, they boarded another bus. "It goes right to your hotel," said the driver. "Straight to the White Swan."

Howard Suzuki laughed. "The White Swan Express!"

By the time they arrived at the White Swan Hotel, they were exhausted. They got their keys, found their rooms, and fell into bed.

Across the city at the orphanage, Wu Li, Li Shen, Qian Ye, and Chun Mei Ni had their last diaper change of the day.

"Tomorrow will be your special day," whispered the aunties as they changed the babies. Then they bundled them in warm blankets and put them to bed.

Wu Li slept on her back with her arms stretched wide like the branches of a tree.

Li Shen snuggled on her side.

Qian Ye slept curled in a ball.

And Chun Mei Ni rolled over and smiled in her sleep.

The next morning there was a thick fog and gray drizzle as dawn came to the city of Guangzhou. At the White Swan Hotel the travelers from North America brushed their teeth, took their showers, combed their hair, and then got dressed. They checked their bags, checked their papers, and went to breakfast. Everyone had *congee*, which is rice porridge, and tea.

Across the city at the orphanage the aunties woke the babies and got them ready. Each was told, "Today is the special day. You will meet your new family."

"*Zhe shi yi ge te bie de ri zi,*" said the aunties. "*Nimen yao hui jian nimen xin de jia ting.*"

As they boarded the bus to the government building, the aunties said, "*Baobei men, zhu nimen jin tian hao yun qi,*" which means, "Good fortune today, sweet babies."

19

At the White Swan Hotel the seven travelers left their rooms and walked down the hall, down the stairs, and into the lobby. Judy Chen was waiting for them. She had come from the orphanage to take them to meet their daughters.

20

Out they went into the foggy morning behind Judy Chen. At an open market, they stopped and bought silver bracelets with silver bells for their babies.

The street was crowded with bicycles as they followed Judy Chen to the government building. At first they laughed and talked. But as they got closer, they began to get quiet. They were even quieter as they entered the building. And quieter still when they went up the stairs and into the room where they would wait.

A hush fell as they took their seats, and the room was as silent as still water.
But their hearts thumped like drums and fluttered like the wings of a bird.

They waited and waited. It seemed like forever. But then, finally, one by one, their daughters came.

Beth and Lewis Maynard met Wu Li.

Andrea Lee and Charlotte Appleford met Li Shen.

Rebecca Mandel met Qian Ye.

Jessica and Howard Suzuki met Chun Mei Ni.

At last they held their babies. They smiled and laughed. Then Charlotte
Appleford cried, tears of joy. So did Howard Suzuki.

Next they fed their daughters.
It was as if they'd always been theirs.

27

Then, after signing all the papers, which took a long time, they left with their babies. As they walked down the street in the city of Guangzhou in the province of Guangdong, the fog began to lift and the sun broke through the mist.

28

"This is the first sun we've seen in weeks," said the shopkeeper as they passed.
"It means good fortune!"

29

Two months later, in North America, it was the holiday season. As they had promised before they left China, the friends from the White Swan Express sent each other cards.

PEACE LOVE & JOY
from the Maynards - Lewis, Beth, and Alicia Wu Li

Alicia Wu Li 2 yrs 3/4

merry christmas
From our family to yours

Andrea Lee, Charlotte Appleford & Molly Li Shen Lee Appleford.

Happy Hanukkah from Rebecca & Rachel Qian Ye Mandel & Ralph

Ralph

Happy Holidays from the Suzuki family
Howard, Jessica, and Emily Chun Mei Ni Suzuki!

For the lunar New Year, the families again sent cards, as they would every year for years to come. With the cards came photos of their daughters. Each daughter wore the bracelet with the silver bell the families had bought together that very special morning in the city of Guangzhou in the province of Guangdong, in China. And on each of the cards it said, in Chinese—Happy New Year! *Gung Hay Fat Choy!*

This story is based on Dr. Elaine M. Aoki and her husband's experiences of becoming a family. The Chinese government's policy that couples can have only one child means that many children are available for adoption, most of them girls. Many people from North America make the long journey to their children in China. But first the family has to complete adoption-agency paperwork, have interviews, fill out legal forms, and receive approvals. Then a tiny photograph of their child arrives. Finally, they travel to China, going to the city nearest the Chinese orphanage to embrace their long-awaited child.

The new family will spend up to two weeks in China. In the child's birth province they obtain an official adoption certificate, a birth certificate, and medical records, a process that takes four to seven days. Then, no matter which province their child is adopted from, all families must go to Guangzhou (GOO-ahng-JO), which is where all foreign embassies are located. They stay in Guangzhou for four to seven more days while they receive the visas, green cards, and passports their children will need to exit the country.

While they are in China, many families take photos and collect books and mementos that they hope will give their child a sense of pride and connection to his or her ethnic and cultural heritage. A silver bracelet with silver bells is often included. Traditionally, a Chinese girl is given at birth a silver bracelet with silver bells, so that her parents can keep track of her when she begins to explore.

Each infant in a Chinese orphanage is assigned a caretaker or nanny. Some older children still live in orphanages, waiting to be adopted, and it was they who told us that the caretakers are affectionately called "auntie," *ayi* in Chinese.

Most of the Chinese phrases used in this book are Mandarin, the official language of China. The New Year's greeting at the end, *Gung Hay Fat Choy,* is Cantonese, used here because it is commonly used by Chinese in North America. Chinese New Year is celebrated according to the lunar calendar and falls in either January or February.

The Chinese now use a system known as *pinyin,* officially adopted in 1958, to write their language using the Roman alphabet. A *q* at the beginning of a word is pronounced more or less like *ch* in English, and an *x* sounds more or less like *s.*